Deleted

NIU Press is pleased to work with the P-20 Center at Northern Illinois University to publish a series of STEM-based storybooks for young readers.

The P-20 Center collaborates with university and community partners to promote innovation in teaching and learning, and foster educational success for all ages.

The Stuffed Bunny Science Adventure Series for young readers is an extension of STEM Read, a P-20 program that helps readers explore the science, technology, engineering, and math concepts behind popular fiction.

This series shares the adventures of a fluff-brained bunny named Bear and his favorite boy, Jack. In each story, Bear meets other toys who teach him about the world around him. The books explore the importance of working together and making friends. They also incorporate STEM concepts aligned with the Next Generation Science Standards. Learn more about the Stuffed Bunny Science Adventure Series and find resources, videos, and games at stemread.com.

SCIENCE · TECHNOLOGY
ENGINEERING · MATH
STEMREAD
NORTHERN ILLINOIS UNIVERSITY

P-20 Center

NIU
PRESS

Northern Illinois University Press, DeKalb 60115

© 2015 by Northern Illinois University

24 23 22 21 20 19 18 17 16 15   1 2 3 4 5

978-0-87580-496-5 (cloth)

978-1-60909-192-7 (ebook)

Library of Congress Cataloging-in-Publication Data

is available online at http://catalog.loc.gov

Printed in China

Production Date: August 2015

Plant & Location: Printed by Shenzhen Caimei Printing Co. Ltd., Shenzhen City, China

Job/Batch # 54155-0

The Toy
and the
TWISTER

A Stuffed Bunny Science Adventure

By Gillian King-Cargile
Illustrations by Kevin Krull

NORTHERN ILLINOIS UNIVERSITY PRESS

One hot, humid day, a stuffed bunny named Bear sat in a sandbox playing with his favorite boy, Jack.

The sky was yellow and hazy. The air was thick with heat, and Bear was glad that he was made of cool fabric fluff instead of plastic.

"Bear!" Jack yelled. "Countdown to adventure!" Jack scooped Bear up in his arms and ran to the middle of the yard. Bear knew that when Jack started counting down, something fantastic was about to happen.

"Three, two, one, BLASTOFF!" Jack launched Bear straight up into the air.

The breeze blew gently through Bear's floppy fabric ears and ruffled his puffball tail. "I'm an astronaut! I'm headed to the moon!" Bear cried, but Jack didn't hear him because Bear could only speak Toy.

Bear saw dark clouds approaching. The clouds hung so low that he thought he could almost reach them and pull some puffy gray mist into his paw.

But gravity had other plans, and Bear fell into
Jack's waiting arms, where he always felt safe.

Jack threw Bear again and again. The little stuffed bunny pretended he was a flying trapeze artist, a sky diver, a fighter pilot.

But around Bear and his boy, the sky grew greeny-blue and grumbly with thunder.

Jack's older sister Sophie called from the
porch. "There's a tornado warning, Jackie. Mom
says you have to come inside."

Jack and Bear ran farther into the yard. "I'm not Jackie. I'm NASA Mission Control and I'm sending you to Mars!"

"I'm going to be the first bunny on Mars!" Bear cheered.

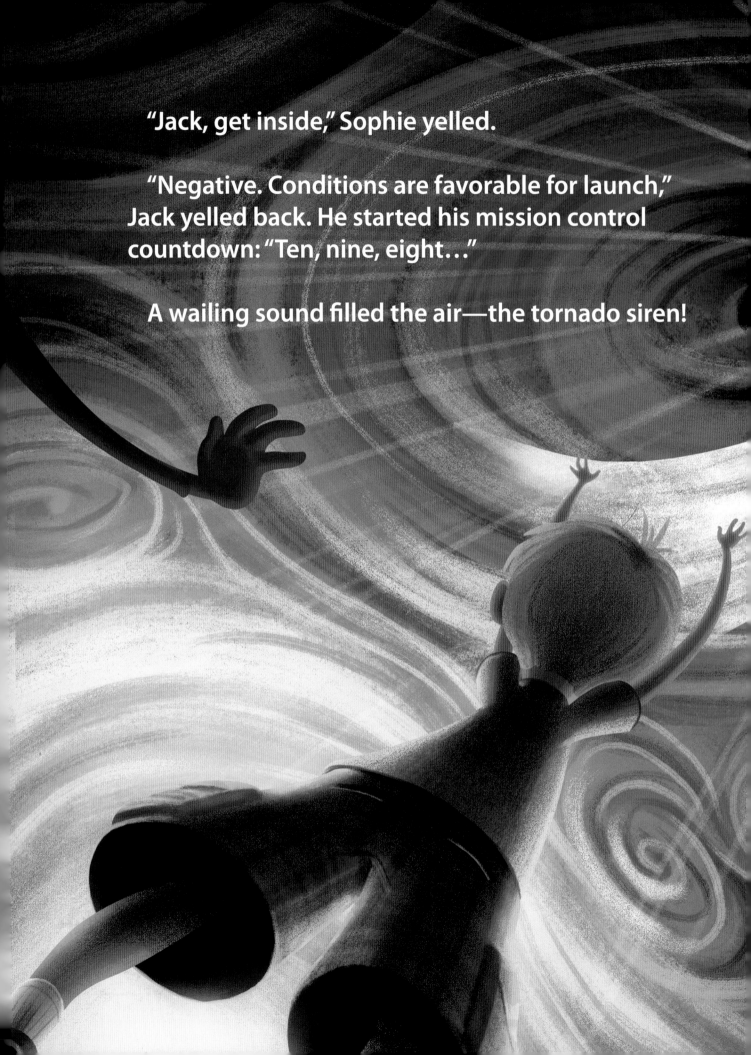

"Jack, get inside," Sophie yelled.

"Negative. Conditions are favorable for launch," Jack yelled back. He started his mission control countdown: "Ten, nine, eight…"

A wailing sound filled the air—the tornado siren!

"We have to launch early!" Jack hugged Bear. "Good luck, friend!" Jack threw Bear as high as he could.

Bear soared into the approaching storm. Before he could land safely in Jack's arms, Sophie grabbed Jack.

"I have to get Bear!" Jack yelled.

"We have to get to the basement!" Sophie dropped her Sadie Scientist doll to the ground and pulled Jack into the house.

"Jack, don't leave me!" Bear yelled, but his tiny toy voice was drowned out by the siren and the wind.

Bear flopped to the ground. He was outside all alone. "I'm done for!" he cried.

A small plastic hand yanked him by the ear. "You're not done for, Fluff Brain."

It was Sophie's Sadie Scientist doll. "Did you get left outside, too?" Bear asked.

"Of course not! Sophie and I are conducting a weather experiment."

The clouds around them started to swirl.
"A funnel cloud!" Sadie cheered. Frozen chunks
of hail pelted the ground. "Assume the storm
position!" she cried. Sadie crouched down and
folded her jointed plastic arms over her head.

"Why?" Bear asked.

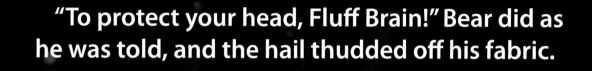

"To protect your head, Fluff Brain!" Bear did as he was told, and the hail thudded off his fabric.

Sadie yelled over the storm, "The best place to be in a storm is a basement or a bathroom on the lowest floor of the house."

Bear wished he was safe inside with Jack.

In the field behind Jack's yard, the storm cloud seemed to reach down to touch the earth with a pointy, swirling finger.

"We're about to get swept up into the tornado!" Sadie yelled.

Sadie grabbed one of Bear's floppy ears. "How well is this stitched on?" Before Bear could answer, Sadie knotted his ear around her arm, and the twirling twister lifted the two of them into the air.

Bear and Sadie flew through the air, turning around and around with the dirt and branches the storm had ripped out of the field. The tornado was loud, like thunder that wouldn't stop thundering.

Some of the shingles from Jack's roof went flying toward Bear. But he breathed a sigh of relief as the tornado veered away from Jack's house.

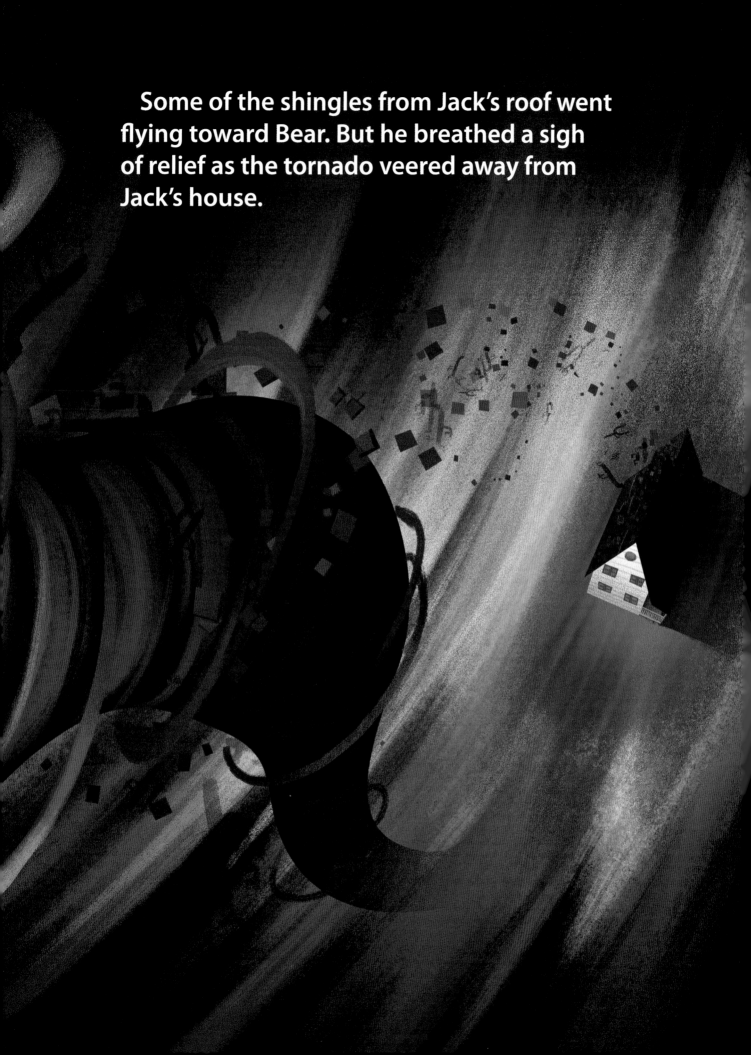

"This is scientastic!" Sadie yelled. "We're actually in the vortex."

"The what?"

"The column of spinning air that makes up a tornado, Fluff Brain!"

Now that Jack was safe, Sadie's excitement started to rub off on Bear. "We're going race-car fast!" he yelled.

Sadie looked at the debris flying around them. "The storm isn't strong enough to pick up cars or pull trees out of the ground. I'm guessing it's a weak tornado, an EF1 on the Enhanced Fujita Scale."

"I'm getting dizzy now," groaned Bear.

"You should be," Sadie yelled. "We're spinning superfast, like water circling a bathtub drain."

"Jack doesn't take me in the tub," said Bear. "I'm too fluffy." Bear missed his boy and was ready for the storm to be over.

All of a sudden, the winds died down and blew away. Gravity took over, and Bear and Sadie started to fall.

Sadie screamed. "Fluff Brain, I'm scared! I'm hard plastic. I'm done for!"

"You're not done for," Bear said. He wrapped his paws around Sadie.

Bear held her on his fluffy tummy. They plopped to the ground and bounced safely back into Jack's yard.

"Thanks for saving me, Bear."

Bear smiled at his new friend.

"Maybe I'll see you around the sandbox sometime," Sadie said.

Sophie strode over and shook Sadie's little plastic hand. "Another successful experiment."

"Bear!" Jack yelled. The boy ran to his bunny and pulled him into his arms. Water squished out of Bear's fluffy stuffing and soaked into Jack's shirt. "Did you make it to space? Did you touch Mars?"

"I was a race car driver. A storm chaser. A scientist!" Bear cheered.

Bear knew that Jack didn't speak Toy, but he was sure his boy understood. Jack carried Bear back into the house to get him cleaned up and ready for their next adventure.

ASK AN EXPERT

Douglas Sisterson,
Research Meteorologist, Argonne National Laboratory

Ever wonder what makes the rain fall or the wind blow? Do you like looking out the window during a thunder storm? You might have the makings of a meteorologist.

What's a meteorologist?

Meteorologists are scientists who study the weather. They measure how much rain falls, how hard the wind blows, and how much humidity (water vapor) is in the air. Meteorologists warn people when storms are coming. Their predictions can save lives!

What is the Enhanced Fujita Scale?

Dr. Tetsuya Theodore Fujita created the Fujita Scale in 1971 to rate tornadoes based on the damage they caused. Scientists created the Enhanced Fujita Scale in 2006 to show how storms damage different types of buildings and how storms damage plants and trees in areas without buildings.

What do the EF numbers mean?

The Enhanced Fujita Scale goes from zero to five. A storm with an EF rating of zero might blow a few shingles off the roof of a house. A storm with an EF rating of five could blow away the entire house.

What's the difference between a funnel cloud and a tornado?

A funnel cloud is a swirling mass of clouds that does not touch the ground. When strong, swirling winds exist at ground level, the storm is a tornado.

What is a vortex?

Sadie had it right; the vortex is the column of spinning air that makes up a tornado.

What is a tornado watch?

Meteorologists can predict conditions that create tornadoes, but they can't predict exactly when and where tornadoes will form. Meteorologists announce a tornado watch to tell where storms with tornadoes could form during a time range. Then, they use weather radar to watch for rotating winds.

What is a tornado warning?

Weather radar can detect rotating winds (or tornadic activity) in a thunderstorm about thirteen minutes before the vortex forms and touches the ground. When meteorologists detect tornadic activity (or trained weather spotters see it), they issue a tornado warning for the area. While all tornadoes begin with rotating thunderstorms, not all rotating thunderstorms produce tornadoes.

When does the tornado siren go off?

Tornado sirens sound when meteorologists issue a tornado warning for your area. When you hear a tornado siren, take shelter just like Jack and Sophie did in the story.

What if your town doesn't have tornado sirens?

The NOAA Weather Radio is the best warning tool. These radios turn on automatically and sound an alarm to broadcast emergency reports from the National Weather Service.

Why did Sadie say people should take shelter in a bathroom?

If your house does not have a basement, a bathroom on the lowest floor is the best place to take shelter during a storm. Water pipes and drains inside the bathroom walls provide a metal "cage" that is sturdier than an ordinary wall. A closet is the next best place. The rule of thumb is to keep as many walls between you and the tornado as possible.

How did Sadie and Bear end up back in Jack's yard?

Many people think that wind just blows things away, but because tornadoes spin they can actually pick things up and then fling them backwards as the storm continues to move.

What should readers do if they want to become meteorologists?

Meteorologists use math to calculate everything from weather patterns to wind speeds. They use computers, radar, and other technology to make predictions. Meteorologists also need to write and speak clearly so people understand their reports. If you want to be a meteorologist, keep working hard in school and keep reading about weather!

Find more Stuffed Bunny Science Adventure resources, videos, and games at stemread.com.